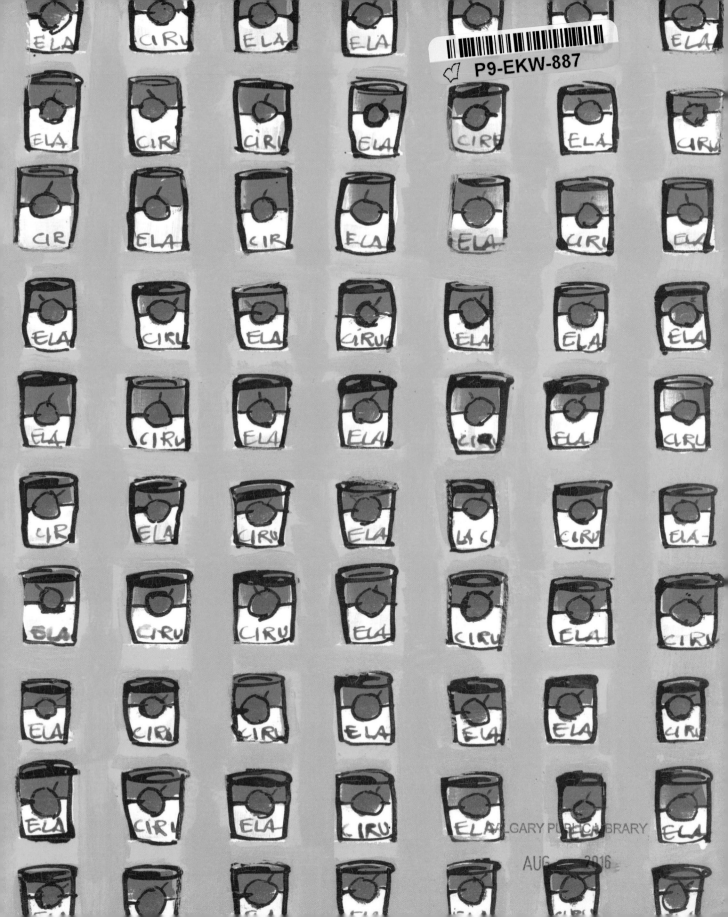

To all those who fight to overcome their fears each day.
To you, who inspired me to write this story.
José Carlos Andrés

For my dear friend Eduardo Zulueta, who fortunately,
and unlike Carlota, has a lot to say, and says it very well.
Emilio Urberuaga

Carlota Wouldn't Say Boo
Somos8 Series

© Text: José Carlos Andrés, 2013
© Images: Emilio Urberuaga, 2014
© Edition: NubeOcho Ediciones, 2014
www.nubeocho.com – info@nubeocho.com

Original title: *Carlota no dice ni pío*
English translation: Robin Sinclair

First edition: September 2014
ISBN: 978 84 942929 5 8
Printed in Spain – Gráficas Jalón

CARLOTA WOULDN'T SAY BOO

JOSÉ CARLOS ANDRÉS
EMILIO URBERUAGA

nubeOCHO

A short time back, just very short, so short that it could have been a second ago, there was a little girl who had a strange power.

That strange power was... was...

Are you ready to know?

It was that she never talked.

Do you think it's strange?

Maybe you don't, because I forgot
to tell you that Carlota didn't
talk because she didn't need to.
Everybody understood her just with
her gestures and glances.

What if she was hungry?

She would just put on her hungry-face
expression and anyone with a ham
sandwich would share it with her.

The same would happen
when she was with her friends.

If at breaktime at school she didn't feel
like running because she was tired,
Carlota would put on a face of

I AM TIRED AND I DON'T FEEL LIKE RUNNING

and everybody would understand her.

And when she was really eager to play a
new game, she would put on a face of

I FEEL LIKE PLAYING A NEW GAME.

And everybody would play with her.

It was a little bit more difficult when the teacher asked her something at school. At that moment, she needed to make a bigger effort, and find a gesture and an expression to answer. But she always managed to do it!

Until one day...

(I open a bracket here to warn you that something very terrifying is about to happen... Before you go on, switch on the light, drink a glass of water with lemon and sugar, and cross your fingers. The last thing is useless, but it is funnier to turn the page this way).

Until one day...

Carlota was chasing her friend Tom the mouse and she ran into the pantry to look for him. Suddenly there was a draught of air and...

¡BANG!

The door suddenly slammed shut.

The little girl was locked in.

Alone.

(Didn't I warn you that something terrifying was about to happen?)

WELL, Carlota thought,

I WILL PUSH THE DOOR AND I WILL BE ABLE TO GET OUT.

But it was impossible to open the pantry from the inside.

She was shut inside that room full of jars, cans and pots.... and a broomstick full of fluff!!

WELL,
Carlota thought again trying to get calmer.

NO BIG DEAL, I WILL LOOK AT SOMEONE AND SEEK HELP.

But Carlota was completely alone.
Without her mom, without her dad
and without Tom the mouse.

Alone, alone, alone... She was alone.

(Yes, I know I have already
said this, but the fact is that:
SHE WAS ALOOONE!!!).

Until that moment, Carlota had never realized that
she did not like being alone at all.

She got nervous and a little afraid, so
she decided then to stare at a tomato can
with her face of

HEY, TOMATO CAN,

HELP ME OPEN THE DOOR BECAUSE I'M AFRAID.

But the tomato can was
a simple tomato can, (though a very high quality)
and it did not understand her.

When she was tired of staring
at the tomato can, she did the
same thing with a plum jam jar,
changing the face of

HEY, TOMATO CAN,
HELP ME OPEN THE DOOR BECAUSE I'M AFRAID,

into the face of

HEY, PLUM JAM JAR, HELP ME OPEN THE DOOR,
BECAUSE I'M VERYYY AFRAID OF BEING LOCKED IN HERE.

But the jar did not understand her either.

Her powers did not work
with the cans and the jars.
With the broomstick, Carlota
did not even try.

At that moment her body started to shake.

She shook more than a milk shake.
She shook so much that all that was
in the pantry shook with her.

Carlota realized she had to try
something she had never done
until now: **Talk.**

IT SHOULD NOT BE SO DIFFICULT, she thought.

She breathed in deeply and opened
her mouth to speak, but only a light
puff came out, and not a single sound.

So Carlota then took in a very
deep breath, filled her lungs with
way too much air, until she finally
managed to whisper:

– MOM, DAD, TOM; I AM LOCKED INSIDE THE PANTRY...

The tomato can
and the plum jam jar stared
at Carlota. We are not sure if
the broomstick stared at her
too, because it was covered
with fluff and it was not
easy to see its eyes!

Carlota breathed in much deeper
and yelled:

– PAAANTRY!!!

Tom the mouse, who was jumping from
one step to another one, remained frozen
in the air. The flies stopped buzzing and
the flowers paused their growth.

No one had ever heard
such a beautiful, **sweet**
and **colorful voice** before.

Carlota yelled even louder:

– MOM! DAD! TOM! I AM LOCKED INSIDE THE PAAANTRY!!!

Mom was reading and the letters from
her book jumped up to the ceiling.

Dad was listening to music and the
notes dropped down to the ground.

The neighbors from the nearby
houses, the neighbors from the
nearby villages, and the neighbors
from those **villages** that were not so
close, but far far away, all listened with
their mouths open when they heard a voice
which was so **colorful,** so **sweet** and so
beautiful (there were even some who
swallowed some of the flies that
had stopped buzzing).

Following that colorful trail of a voice,
Dad, Mom and Tom the mouse opened
the pantry door.

There was Carlota, with an expression
on her face that read:

I WAS SO AFRAID BEING ALONE.

But this time they did not understand
her. She searched for her best gesture
to express herself again without words:

I WAS SOOO AFRAID BEING ALONE.

But they still did not understand her.

So, Carlota took a deep breath, and
making a huge effort again, she said:

– THANK YOU.

Mom, Dad and Tom the mouse put
on a "you're welcome" face. And all of
them laughed together.

Carlota told them what had happened.
Slowly at the beginning, but the more
she talked, the more she was feeling
comfortable.

I WAS VERY SCARED BECAUSE I FELT COMPLETELY ALONE.
BUT THEN IT WAS NOT REALLY TRUE, I WAS WITH MYSELF
AND YOU WERE NEARBY.

And after she had narrated
everything that had occurred, she
decided to continue telling them
lots and lots of things that she had
never told them before.

(NOw I am telling you a **secret** that you can tell no one. And I will **whisper** it to you so that you will be the only one to know it: FROM THAT DAY **ON**, CARLOTA WAS NEVER **EVER** AFRAID, BECAUSE SHE KNEW SHE WAS WITH **HERSELF,** AND THAT HER PARENTS WERE NE**ARBY).**

What nobody ever knew was that she still talked with her friend, Tom the mouse, without words, using only her gestures and glances.

And they understood each other perfectly well.

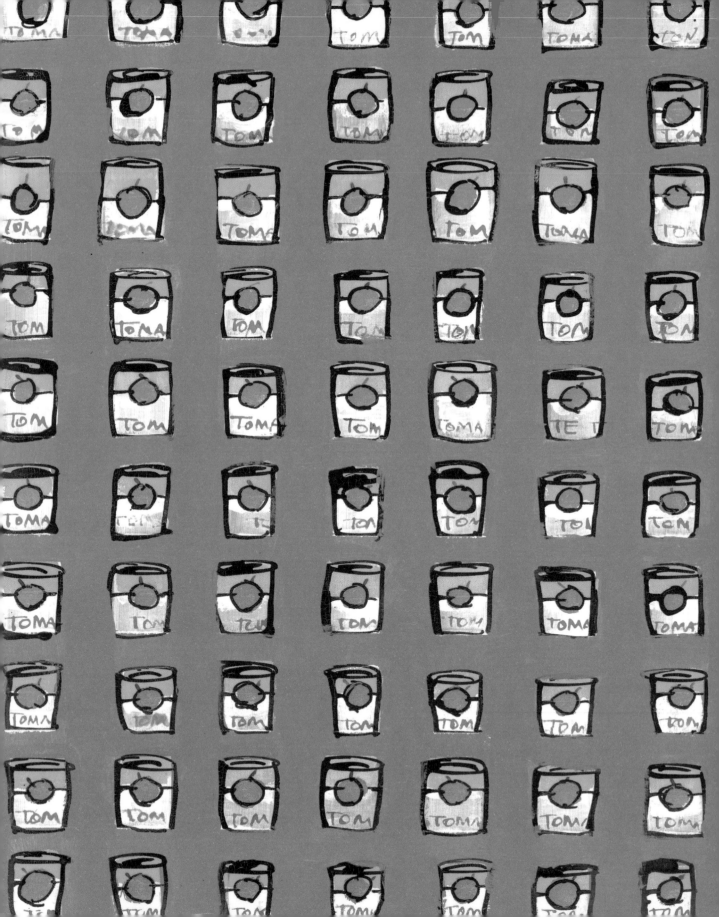